Disney's
Aladdin
DON'T BUG THE GENIE!

by Page McBrier

**Illustrations by
Raymond Zibach and Kenny Thompkins**

ISBN 1-56326-250-9

CHAPTER 1

he sun beat down on the desert. All was quiet. And peaceful. And hot.

Inside the Sultan's palace, Aladdin was taking a nap after lunch. His pet monkey, Abu, was tucked under his arm. Jasmine lay on the divan. The Magic Carpet had rolled itself up, and the Genie snored peacefully near a window, his sapphire glistening in his navel.

Aladdin and Jasmine lived in the Royal Palace with Jasmine's father, the Sultan, Abu, and the Magic Carpet. Aladdin had become a prince when the Genie granted him his first wish. When Aladdin set the Genie free, they became good friends.

As they were sleeping, a big, hairy bug with emerald-green eyes flew through the window and dropped quietly onto the floor.

It scooted past Aladdin and Jasmine.

Then the bug stopped, waved its feathered antennae, and headed straight for the Genie.

Buzzing softly, the bug crawled up the Genie's leg toward his stomach. It gazed at the sapphire, then grabbed it and ran down the Genie's leg.

When the Genie started to sit up, the bug dropped the sapphire onto a pillow on the floor. *Chomp!* It bit the Genie.

"Owwwww!" The Genie slapped his leg. Sparks and puffs of blue smoke filled the air.

The bug grabbed the sapphire again and flew out the window.

"What's going on?" cried Aladdin.

"A bug bit me!" shouted the Genie. "Ow, ow, ow, ow!" He bounced around the room.

Abu tugged on Aladdin's pants and pointed out the window, but Aladdin ignored him.

"Are you okay, Genie?" asked Jasmine.

The Genie turned yellow, then purple.

He burped — loud.

Aladdin had never seen the Genie like this. He was usually blue — and more polite. Aladdin shook his head. "You can't be this sick from a bug bite."

Violet bubbles popped out of the Genie's mouth. He grabbed Aladdin's shoulder. "I'm dizzy." He spun around. "Whoa! Easy, boy."

"Watch out for the table!" cried Jasmine.

Boom! The Genie sprawled across the rug. He burped again. "Sorry, folks."

"It's okay," said Aladdin.

The Genie rubbed his leg. "That little critter had some set of chompers."

Aladdin helped the Genie stand up. Jasmine rubbed the Genie's leg with lotion. "Try to get some rest," she said.

"Good idea," said the Genie. Magenta steam popped out of his ears and swirled around his feet. "Uh-oh."

"What's wrong?" asked Aladdin.

The Genie searched the floor. "My new sapphire. It's missing."

"You mean that big blue thing you had in

your belly button?" said Aladdin.

The Genie touched his navel. "Please — it's my new tummy treasure. My belly bauble. It's the latest style from the Orient. All the genies are wearing them."

"Don't worry," said Aladdin, patting his arm. "It'll turn up."

"I hope so," said the Genie. He put his other arm around Aladdin's shoulder and burped again.

"Has this happened before?" Jasmine asked him.

"Never," said the Genie. His eyes crossed and shut. "It *must* be the bug bite." He leaned against Aladdin's shoulder.

"Jasmine's right. You should rest," said Aladdin.

The Genie flopped down on the rug and folded his hands over his chest. "I'm sure I'll be fine by tomorrow. I'll look for the sapphire then." He closed his eyes and fell asleep.

"What kind of bug could make the Genie so sick?" Aladdin asked Jasmine.

She shook her head. "I don't know, but he

sure doesn't look good."

Abu jumped up and down and pointed out the window, but again no one paid any attention to him.

CHAPTER 2

he next morning, the Genie was up early.

"Rise and shine, Al, my man," he said.

Aladdin opened one eye. "How are you feeling?"

The Genie held out his arm. "Still purple with a touch of yellow. And still no sapphire." He burped a purple bubble.

Aladdin sat up. "I think you've got something on your face now, too."

"Pimples?" the Genie said. "I thought I got rid of those five hundred years ago!"

"No, no," said Aladdin. "Blotches. Purple and yellow blotches. They look kind of slimy." He leaned forward. "In fact, your whole body looks slimy."

The Genie touched his face, then his chest. His fingers got coated with sticky ooze. "Eeeuuu. I'm melting."

Abu scooted to the far side of Aladdin's bed. Even Aladdin moved back. "Maybe some breakfast would help."

"Maybe," said the Genie. "Allow me, your Princeness." He rubbed his gooey hands together. "For our dining pleasure, a platter of fresh fruit. Perhaps some oranges...dates... figs." He snapped his fingers as best he could.

A silver tray appeared on his palm. The Genie sighed happily. "See that? At least part of me still works."

He lifted the lid on the tray. "Aaaaa!"

The Genie threw the tray full of beetles into the air. They scattered to the corners of the room. "Oh, boy! What do you say we order take-out instead?" said the Genie.

"Genie! What's happening to you?" asked Aladdin.

"I don't know, Al. I was fine until that bug

bit me." Purple steam flowed from his ears. "Help! I'm going to self-destruct!"

"Let's not panic," said Aladdin. "I'm taking you to Fatima. Now."

"Who?"

"Fatima. She's a healer."

"Has she treated many genies?"

"I'm not sure," said Aladdin. He unrolled the Magic Carpet. But it curled itself back up with a snap. "What's wrong with you, Carpet?"

"I think it's my slime," the Genie whispered. "Or maybe my burps."

The Carpet wound itself even tighter.

"Never mind. We'll walk," said Aladdin. "Coming, Abu?" Abu shook his head. So Aladdin led the Genie through the palace, down the grand staircase, and out into the courtyard, where they met Jasmine.

When Jasmine saw the Genie, she stared at him hard. "You are definitely not better. What you are is a big sticky mess!" she said.

The Genie lifted his arm. The morning sun shone down on his skin. *Drip. Drip.* "Just like a giant melting crayon," he said.

Jasmine wrinkled her nose. "Genie, you're not even funny anymore." Then Aladdin told her about Fatima.

The Genie turned to Aladdin. "I'll get us a camel," he said. He snapped his fingers.

"No, no, that's okay —" said Aladdin. But it was too late. Aladdin shot into the air. A wild goat ran under him, and he landed on its back.

"Hold on, Al!" yelled the Genie.

The goat took off across the courtyard with Aladdin holding on. "Yeow!" cried Aladdin, bouncing along. They bolted through the gates and toward the marketplace. "Help!"

The marketplace was crowded. "Watch out!" Aladdin shouted. He grazed a woman carrying a jar on her head.

Aladdin and the goat zigzagged around long tables stacked with bread, cloth, and dishes. They crashed into a table piled with oranges. Aladdin slid off the goat. "Sorry," he said to the merchant. He picked up the

oranges and handed him a gold coin.

The goat ran away, and Aladdin walked —
limping — back to the palace.

Jasmine shook her head as he came into
the courtyard. "This has gone too far," she
said, and she hurried inside.

"No more genie magic," Aladdin said.

Jasmine returned with a long hooded robe.
"I hope Fatima can help. At least this will
keep him from scaring anyone," she said.

"Aren't you coming?" asked Aladdin.

"You're better with sick genies. Besides, I
don't want to be around if he gets worse," said
Jasmine. She called to the Magic Carpet and
Abu. "Come down here, you two. Aladdin
and the Genie need your help."

The Carpet slunk out the door. Abu
followed behind. "Thanks, Jasmine," said
Aladdin. He, Abu, and the Genie climbed
aboard the Carpet. "I promise we won't come
back until he's blue again."

Jasmine waved good-bye. "Good luck," she
said. "You're going to need it."

CHAPTER 3

etting to Fatima's house was tricky. Aladdin, Abu, and the Genie wound their way through the crowded marketplace on the Magic Carpet, past busy shops and houses. Finally they reached a dusty, crooked street on the edge of the desert. "Almost there," said Aladdin.

"Good," said the Genie. "How do I look?"

"Don't ask," said Aladdin.

At the end of the street stood a small house. A spindly olive tree grew in front of it, and a heavy curtain covered the doorway. The Carpet landed.

"Fatima! Are you home?" called Aladdin.

"Depends," a voice called back.

"It's Aladdin, Fatima. Remember me?"

A tall, stout woman stuck her head out the door. She had a round, shiny face and wore bracelets on each arm.

"Ah, yes! The beggar boy I once cured. You'd eaten too many olives." She eyed his clothes. "Have you come into some money, Aladdin?"

"Actually, I came into a genie," Aladdin answered.

"You always were a clever one," she said. "What can I do for you?"

Aladdin pushed the Genie forward and peeled back his hood.

Fatima's eyes grew dark. "Is that your genie? Doesn't look too good."

"He's sick. His powers have gotten all mixed up," Aladdin answered.

"I don't do genies," she said. "Only camels, elephants, monkeys, and people."

"But Fatima..."

"No exceptions." She turned and disappeared behind the curtain.

The Genie slumped against Fatima's house. "I'm washed up. A broken genie is a worthless genie. I'm a useless, purple blob." A lavender bubble slipped from his mouth and floated past the door. *Pop!* Then another. *Pop!* Aladdin patted his hand, then wiped his fingers on the Genie's robe.

Fatima pulled back the curtain. "Either get that genie out of here or put a bucket under him."

"But I know you can help him," said Aladdin. He smiled. "Please, Fatima? A great and powerful healer like you?"

"Heh, heh, heh." As Fatima laughed, her jewelry bounced up and down. She looked at the Genie. "Well, what can you pay me?"

"Bubbles?" said the Genie. *Pop! Pop! Pop!*

"Three gold coins," said Aladdin.

"Six," said Fatima.

Aladdin folded his arms. "Five."

Fatima shook her head. "No deal."

"I knew it," said the Genie. "You may as well ship me back to the Cave of Wonders."

"Okay, six," said Aladdin. "Don't be silly,

Genie. You're worth it." He started to pat the Genie on the back again, then changed his mind.

"Bring the Genie inside and take off his robe," ordered Fatima. "The monkey and the rug can wait outside."

The Genie took up most of the room inside Fatima's house. It was filled with strange bottles and potions on the shelves. A faded rug lay on the floor.

"Stand still," Fatima said to the Genie. "I don't want a mess in here." She made him stand on an old cloth and then studied him from top to bottom. "Ummmm. Doesn't look good. Tell me what happened."

The Genie explained about the bug bite.

"Ummmm," said Fatima. "Gooey." She poked the Genie's cheeks and looked inside his ears.

"Can you heal him?" asked Aladdin.

"Nope," said Fatima.

"Doomed!" wailed the Genie.

Fatima's eyes glittered. "I can tell you what

will, though. Heh, heh, heh."

Aladdin and the Genie waited.

"Your genie got bitten by a jewel bug," Fatima said. "Very rare."

"'A jewel bug'? What's that?" asked Aladdin.

"Looks like a bumblebee with big emerald eyes," Fatima replied. "Its bite causes people to look and behave strangely."

"Great," said Aladdin.

"Did you have any jewels lying around?" Fatima went on. "That's probably what it was after. It collects jewels."

The Genie let out another wail. "My new tummy trinket! I bet that sneaky critter stole my big blue sapphire."

Fatima lifted her eyebrows. "I'm very fond of sapphires myself. Especially big ones. Heh, heh, heh."

"That's my belly bauble," said the Genie. "It's not for sale. N-O. No way."

Fatima waved the Genie off. "Very well." She turned to Aladdin. "To cure your genie, you must do two things. First, you must find the jewel bug."

"Where?" asked Aladdin.

"That I can't help you with," said Fatima.

The Genie groaned. "Six gold coins for this?"

"Once you find the bug," Fatima went on, "you must dip its antennae in the Well of Forgetfulness. Then rub the antennae across the Genie's forehead.

"The well of what? Never heard of it," said Aladdin.

Fatima went over to the corner and rummaged through a box. "Aha!" She held up a round, dusty object. "This may come in handy." She dusted it off with the corner of her skirt.

"A compass?" said Aladdin.

Fatima pressed it into his hand. "Not just any compass. This one is magic. It will always point you in the direction you wish to go.

"And know this," she added. "Your time gets shorter by the hour. The Genie and his powers grow ever weaker."

"Let me get this straight," the Genie said.

"My powers are about to go kaput, we don't *know* where we're going, and you expect me to trust my life to a compass!"

"Try it," said Fatima. "Heh, heh, heh."

"What choice do we have, Genie?" said Aladdin.

"Tell me about choices, Al," said the Genie. "I feel like a candy bar in a hot oven. Is this my choice? I don't mind the purple color so much, but the dripping...the dripping is really getting me down."

CHAPTER 4

et's try the compass," said Aladdin. He ran out to the far side of Fatima's yard with Abu and the Magic Carpet. "I wish to go to Fatima the Healer's house," he told the compass. The needle spun around, stopped, and pointed to the house. "Bull's-eye!" Aladdin shouted.

Fatima poked her head out of the doorway and grinned. Her gold tooth sparkled. "What did you expect? Heh, heh, heh."

Fatima tossed the Genie's robe out the door. "Now give me my gold and get this melting mess out of my yard."

Aladdin placed six gold coins in Fatima's

palm. Holding the magic compass he said, "We wish to find the jewel bug."

The needle trembled for a moment, then pointed west. "Let's go," said Aladdin.

The Carpet circled the Genie warily.

"Stop sulking," Aladdin said to it. "The sooner we find that bug, the better for all of us." He spread the robe over the Carpet like a blanket for the Genie to sit on. "Hop aboard, everyone."

"Good-bye, Fatima," he called.

The Magic Carpet flew over Fatima's house and out into the desert. "Hang onto your turbans," Aladdin said. "We're on our way."

A stream of lilac-colored bubbles escaped from the Genie's mouth. "Can we stop a minute, Al?" The Genie cupped his hand over his mouth.

"You're not carpet-sick, are you?"

"No. I'll be okay."

Aladdin kept his eyes on the compass. "Go left," he told the Carpet when the needle changed. "Now right."

The Carpet flew on and on, over villages, a

caravan, and two herds of wild horses.

"Are we there yet?" asked the Genie.

Aladdin looked at Abu, who was leaning over the edge of the Carpet. "Nope."

The Genie moaned.

The Carpet kept going. The afternoon light turned the desert pink. Soft winds blew wavy patterns across the sand, and the air grew chilly.

"It'll be dark before too long," said Aladdin. He peeked at the Genie, who had turned the color of grape juice.

The desert was now behind them. Golden peaks, higher than anything Aladdin had ever seen, rose before them. Aladdin checked the compass. "Straight ahead," he told the Carpet.

"Are you sure it wants us in those mountains?" said the Genie.

The Carpet flew on. Now the mountains were only a short distance away. "There's nothing here but little bitty bushes," said the Genie.

They scooted between two of the highest peaks and kept going.

The mountains blocked the sun. Abu gripped Aladdin's arm.

The Carpet began to move forward in fits and starts.

"Hey, watch it!" the Genie told the Carpet. "This isn't helping my indigestion."

"You're doing fine," Aladdin told it in a soothing voice.

The needle spun sharply. "To the right," said Aladdin.

The Magic Carpet stopped. "What's wrong?" cried the Genie, falling backward.

They were hovering in front of a mountain cave.

Aladdin rechecked the compass. "We wish to find the jewel bug," he told it. The needle stayed still. "Hmm," said Aladdin. "I hope this compass knows what it's doing."

CHAPTER 5

hey stared at the opening. "Pretty creepy, pal," said the Genie.

Aladdin frowned. "We're going in. There's no time to waste."

The Genie cleared his throat. "Right. That creepy crawler owes me big time."

"Let's go," said Aladdin. The Carpet edged forward.

Abu covered his eyes as they moved inside.

Aladdin took a deep breath. The cave smelled like a room full of wet towels.

"Phew!" said the Genie, fanning the air. He leaned to one side and peered farther into the cave.

"See anything?" asked Aladdin.

"A long tunnel," said the Genie. "A very long, *dark* tunnel."

The Carpet slowed down.

"Sorry," Aladdin said. "The compass says to keep going. Maybe the jewel bug likes dark places." He scanned the tunnel for a pair of glittering green eyes.

The Genie grabbed his arm. "What's that?"

Aladdin jumped. "Where?"

Abu scrambled onto Aladdin's shoulder and put his hands over his eyes. "Easy, Abu. You're blocking my view."

"I thought I saw something behind that big rock," said the Genie.

Aladdin and the Genie leaned forward.

"False alarm," said Aladdin, relaxing. "Abu, sit down and stop pinching my arm."

They moved on.

"Ow!" cried the Genie.

"What? What is it?" said Aladdin. "Do you see something?"

"No. Abu pulled on my beard," said the Genie.

The tunnel twisted to the right and then

to the left, becoming narrower all the time. "I don't like this, buddy boy," said the Genie. "It feels like we're being swallowed up."

"I know," said Aladdin, still searching for a pair of green eyes. "It's so dark I can barely see the compass."

"I can help," said the Genie. "I'll just nod my head once and..."

"No!" said Aladdin.

"But Al, I've got it all figured out," said the Genie. "Not to worry."

"Genie!"

Poof.

"Uh-oh," said the Genie. "My mistake."

"What is it? What happened?"

"I asked for a flame."

Awk! Awk!

Aladdin turned his head. "What's that squawking noise?" The ruckus grew louder. "Do I hear wings flapping?" He reached around and felt something feathery with a long, thin neck.

"Flame. Flamingo," said the Genie. "I guess the magic got confused."

"There's a flamingo on this carpet?"

Abu began to tug on Aladdin's arm.

"Don't worry. I'll fix it," said the Genie.

The Carpet bucked. Abu screeched.

"Stop it, everyone!" said Aladdin. He took a deep breath. "Be still."

The sides of the tunnel were so close that Aladdin could touch them. "We'll get rid of the flamingo later."

"Forget about the flamingo," said the Genie. "I think I see a light."

"Where?"

"Right above your head."

Aladdin looked up. "You're right," he said. Then he stretched up and pressed his eye to the hole. On the other side, a pair of emerald-green eyes stared back at him.

"It's the jewel bug!" Aladdin whispered. The bug waved its long, feathered antennae at Aladdin and buzzed. Between its two front feet sat the Genie's sapphire.

"Hello, little bug," said Aladdin. "Come over here."

The bug edged closer. "That's right," said

Aladdin. He held out a finger.

"Poke your finger right at it, why don't you?" said the Genie. "You're just begging to get bitten."

"Quiet," whispered Aladdin. But he pulled his finger away from the hole. "Come to me, bug. I see you have the Genie's jewel."

The Genie shoved Aladdin aside. "You little thief!" he yelled into the hole. "Thanks to you I look like an eggplant. Give me back my jewel! Give me back my health and my magic!"

The bug skittered backward. Then it buzzed angrily, grabbed the sapphire with its feet, and disappeared into the hole.

CHAPTER 6

hat did you do that for?" said Aladdin. "I almost had it."

Magenta steam blew out of the Genie's ears. "Nobody messes with a genie."

Aladdin pressed his eye against the hole. "It's gone. Now what do we do?" Abu climbed back up onto Aladdin's shoulder and chattered unhappily.

"Sorry, Al," said the Genie. "I guess I got a little carried away." He sat back down with a thud. "Maybe I can try using my powers again."

The flamingo squawked.

Abu made a face at it.

"Are you kidding?" said Aladdin. "In your condition? Fatima was right. You *are* getting worse."

He held the compass up to the light. It was still pointing at the hole into which the bug had disappeared. "Come on out, you little pest."

Then he remembered that under his princely clothes he was still as clever as he'd been when he had to live by his wits.

Wait...his princely clothes! He reached up and felt the front of his turban where a red-violet jewel held a long feather in place.

He pulled off his turban and pushed the jewel in front of the hole. "Oh, jewel bug," he sang. "Look what I have for you. Great, big, and shiny." He shook his turban gently. "Come and get it."

Bzzzz.

Aladdin looked at the Genie and Abu and pressed his finger to his lips. "Shhhh." He sang into the hole again. "Come out, come out, wherever you are."

Bzzz. Bzzz.

Aladdin slowly drew the turban away from the hole. A feathered antenna appeared. Then another. Then two green eyes and the Genie's sapphire.

"Attabug," said Aladdin. "Come on out."

The bug perched itself on the edge of the hole. Its eyes stayed glued on the turban.

"Look at this pretty jewel," he said, gently waving the turban back and forth.

He tilted the turban toward the jewel bug. "Take a closer look."

Squawk! The flamingo stretched its neck and lunged for the bug.

"Hey! What do you think you're doing?" yelled Aladdin.

But it was too late. The bug, holding onto the sapphire, flew out into the tunnel — with the flamingo close behind.

"Follow that flamingo!" cried Aladdin.

The Carpet shot forward. It zigged to the left and then zagged to the right as the tunnel grew narrower still.

"Duck!" shouted the Genie. He and Aladdin and Abu hung on tight. The Carpet swerved through the tunnel.

"Can you see anything?" asked Aladdin.

"Are you kidding?" said the Genie. "I've got my eyes shut."

A loud squawk followed a buzz.

"Listen, flamingo!" called Aladdin. "If you eat our bug, I'll personally see that you're made into a pillow."

The Carpet bumped on. Aladdin didn't think they could squeeze together much tighter. Would they catch the bug before the flamingo did?

"We're gaining!" said the Genie.

Aladdin lifted his head. "You're right." He saw the flamingo up ahead.

The Carpet veered around a corner, and the tunnel grew wide. They were inside a cavern. A stream flowed beneath them.

With eyes as big as walnuts, the flamingo closed in on the bug. "Uh-oh," said Aladdin. "Stay away from our bug."

The flamingo opened its pink and black beak. *Whoosh!* It scooped up the bug, sapphire and all.

"You rascal! You fiend! You big, pink bird brain!" shouted the Genie.

The bird flew off.

"Step on it, Carpet," Aladdin said.

The Carpet flew to the top of the cavern and then all the way to the bottom. Down, up, around, and around, and around they went. "Now I really am carpet-sick," said the Genie, covering his mouth again. Lavender bubbles began to fill the air. *Pop. Pop. Pop.*

"This isn't getting us anywhere," said Aladdin. "Stop."

As soon as they stopped chasing it, the flamingo landed on a tall ledge. The bug was dangling from its beak.

"Now what?" said the Genie, who was turning pale. He shook his fist. "Ooooh. That featherhead has me fuming."

Aladdin pulled a fig from his pocket. "Never give up." He waved it in the air. "Oh, flamingo. I'll trade you," he said.

The flamingo looked away.

Then Aladdin saw Abu. He was climbing up the cavern wall. He crept along where the bird couldn't see him.

Aladdin smiled. Abu was working with him the way he used to in their days on the street.

"How about a pistachio then?" asked Aladdin. "And by the way, did you ever see my impression of a looney bird?"

Aladdin began hopping around, first on one foot, then on the other. "Hoo, hee, hoo, hee!" said Aladdin, flapping his arms. The flamingo looked down from the ledge.

Meanwhile, Abu had reached the ledge. Sneaking up behind the flamingo, he grabbed the bug and the sapphire out of the bird's beak.

The flamingo flapped its wings and lunged at Abu.

Losing his balance, Abu fell against the back of the ledge. The bug popped out of his hand and tumbled toward the ground.

"The bug! It's okay, Abu. I've got it. I've got it." He ran for his target. *Plop!* The jewel bug landed right in Aladdin's turban.

"He's out!" the Genie yelled. "Careful,

now, A-man. That bitty bug packs a big bite."

"No kidding," said Aladdin. He pinched the turban closed so that the bug wouldn't escape.

The flamingo swept off the ledge and circled Aladdin.

"Shoo! Go away," said Aladdin. He pointed to the stream. "Look. There's plenty of food in there."

The flamingo landed and waded into the stream, where it quickly caught a fish.

"Good riddance!" said Aladdin as he watched the flamingo wander downstream.

"Let me look," the Genie said to Aladdin. "Just a little look." He peeked into the turban. "Hey! Where's my belly bauble?"

Abu scrambled down from the ledge with the sapphire still safe in his hand. He ran over and handed it to the Genie.

The Genie turned the sapphire over. "Bu-Bu Baby, you came through for a sick friend." He started to put the jewel back in his belly, then stopped. "On second thought, I think I'll wait."

"Why?" asked Aladdin.

"I've been thinking, Al. This bug business has been a lot of work. From now on, I'm going to save my bauble for special occasions. Genie balls, genie reunions, singles night at the Genie Club..."

"Genie, are you sure? Maybe you'll feel better if you wear it," said Aladdin.

Genie stuck the sapphire deep in his pocket. "A genie's mind is a terrible thing to change." He rubbed his sticky hands. "What's our next move, Your Worthiness?"

Aladdin laughed. "Now all we need to do is get you cured, Genie." He tried to sound confident.

CHAPTER 7

ucking his turban and the jewel bug under his arm, Aladdin took out the compass. "We have no time to waste. Take us to the Well of Forgetfulness."

The needle twisted slowly to the right. "Oh, no! Another tunnel." He pointed to an opening. They flew in, but a minute later they were outside.

"There are those bushes again," said the Genie.

The compass needle flip-flopped. "Hmm," said Aladdin, frowning. "That's strange. Turn around, Carpet."

The Carpet reversed its direction. The

needle flip-flopped again.

Aladdin scratched his head. He searched the ground below but saw nothing but a few rocks and some bushes. Then something moved.

"Over there." He pointed. The Carpet swung low to the ground.

Aladdin held out the compass. "We wish to find the Well of Forgetfulness," he said.

"You've come to the right place," answered a raspy voice.

"Holy turbans!" said the Genie. "There's something under that bush."

"That's no bush," said Aladdin, hopping off the Carpet. "That's a blanket. Here, Genie," he said, handing over the turban. "Hold this while I take a look. No wonder we missed it." The blanket was green and threadbare. It blended into the bushes surrounding it.

Aladdin approached carefully. "Are you the Well of Forgetfulness?" he asked.

A face as wrinkled as an old raisin peered out at him from underneath. "Do I look like a well to you?"

Aladdin raised his eyebrows.

The man began swaying back and forth, chanting in a strange language. "I am Hamoud, keeper of the Well of Forgetfulness," he said. "Aya, aya, hup. Aya, aya, hup."

"No wonder the compass was confused," said Aladdin under his breath.

"To find the well, you must first answer this riddle," said Hamoud. He squeezed his eyes shut. "Hold on. This'll take a minute."

Hamoud's face grew as tight as a fist.

"Two bodies have I,
Though both joined in one.
The longer I stand,
The quicker I run."

Hamoud's face relaxed.

"Is that it?" asked Aladdin.

Hamoud resumed his chanting. "Aya, aya, hup. Aya, aya, hup."

Aladdin walked back to the Carpet.

"What'd he say?" asked the Genie.

Aladdin repeated the riddle.

Abu scratched his head.

"Hmm," said the Genie. He crossed his legs around Aladdin's turban and peeked in. "If the little green jewel thief knows the answer, he's not saying."

Bzzzz.

Aladdin thought and thought and thought. Could it be water? No. A scroll? No. An icicle? No.

"I'm stumped," said the Genie. He yelled over to Hamoud. "Okay, Mr. Riddler. We give up. Besides, we don't really have time for this. We're on kind of a tight schedule."

Hamoud kept on with his chanting.

"I don't think we're allowed to give up," whispered Aladdin.

Abu began hopping up and down and chattering excitedly.

"What is it?" said Aladdin. "What are you trying to tell us?"

Abu reached down and pretended to pluck something out of the ground. He held it to his nose and took a long sniff.

"A flower?" guessed Aladdin.

Abu nodded his head and motioned for

Aladdin to keep guessing.

"Something like a flower?"

Abu put his hand to his ear.

"SOUNDS like 'flower'!" said the Genie.

Nodding again, Abu hopped up and down.

"Power? Shower? Tower?" they both guessed.

Abu shook his head.

"Hand off!" said the Genie. He passed the turban back to Aladdin. "Big Bite is cramping my style. I'm just getting warmed up."

"I know!" said Aladdin. "Hour!"

Abu somersaulted across the sand and applauded.

The Genie hung his head. "I knew that. I was about to guess 'hour.'"

Abu ran over to the Carpet and jerked it off the ground. He rolled it up lengthwise, then pinched in its waist.

Aladdin stared at the way Abu was holding the Carpet. "It looks just like...an hourglass!" he said. "That's it! An hourglass!

"Two bodies have I,
    Though both joined in one.

The longer I stand,
    The quicker I run."
    From six camel-lengths away, Hamoud
stopped chanting. He pulled out a dusty
hourglass from underneath the blanket.
"Come along," he said, turning the hourglass
over to start it fresh. "Time's slipping by."

Chapter 8

amoud stood up and pulled back his hood. Then he handed the hourglass to Aladdin and pointed south.

"That way," he said, "until the sand runs out." He folded himself back up and sat down.

"Thanks. Thanks very much," said Aladdin. "How can we ever repay you?" Then he remembered the magic compass. "Wait." He took it out and handed it to Hamoud. "Maybe you can use this. We don't need it anymore."

Aladdin explained how it worked.

"Ah," said Hamoud. "Perfect! Now I'll be

able to find the hourglass again. Leave it for me beside the Well of Forgetfulness."

"We'll be happy to," said Aladdin.

He and the Genie and Abu hurried over to the Carpet and got on their way.

The sand inside the hourglass fell steadily. It wouldn't take them long to reach the well.

The Carpet flew out of the mountains and back into the desert. Nothing but rolling sand dunes lay before them.

Aladdin watched the sand in the hourglass become a trickle. "Anyone see a well?"

"Not yet," said the Genie, sighing. "And I'm beginning to feel like a big, moldy grape."

"I know," said Aladdin. As the Carpet swung wide around another rolling dune, the last few grains of sand dropped to the bottom of the hourglass.

"Stop!" the Genie said with a cough. "I see something."

"Whew!" said Aladdin, setting the hour-glass down.

Beneath them, all alone in the desert, sat an old stone well.

The Carpet hovered anxiously overhead. Aladdin leaned down. "This can't be right. It doesn't even look like it has any water."

The Carpet landed and everyone stepped off. The well was built close to the ground. Next to it was a rope attached to a leather bucket.

Aladdin grabbed the bucket. "Maybe we should try lowering this."

The Genie leaned to watch over Aladdin's shoulder.

Abu and the Magic Carpet crowded around the other side of the well as Aladdin lowered the bucket as far as it would go.

Plink!

Aladdin pulled up the bucket. It was full of brown sludge.

"Eeeuuu! That looks like I feel," said the Genie. He took a few steps backward.

Aladdin reached into his turban and carefully pulled the jewel bug out by its wings so that it couldn't reach around and bite him. The bug squirmed angrily.

"Cooperate and we'll let you go," Aladdin

said. The bug quieted down. Aladdin lowered the antennae into the sludge.

Bzzzz.

Aladdin waved the bug in the air. "Ready, Genie? Come back here. This is no time to fool around."

The Genie made a face and returned to the well. "Okay, here goes." He bent down and let Aladdin brush his forehead with the bug's antennae.

"Done!" said Aladdin, dropping the bug back into his turban.

"Well?" said the Genie, looking down at himself. "Anything happening?"

Abu shook his head.

The Genie chewed on his finger. "Now?"

"Um..." said Aladdin. Suddenly a string of purple and blue bubbles shot out of the Genie's ears, followed by red steam with a loud pop and whistle. Abu ran over and hid behind Aladdin's leg.

Aladdin gasped. The Genie's entire body turned the color of blueberry sherbet.

Then, like ice melting off a mountain top,

the blueberry color slid away. "I'm molting!" the Genie yelled. Underneath the blueberry color was the Genie's healthy blue.

The Genie looked at himself and let out a whoop. "Would you look at that?"

"Hooray!" cheered Aladdin.

"Now where's that nasty bug?" said the Genie.

Aladdin handed the Genie his turban.

The Genie opened it up. "Okay, Mr. Personality. I'm letting you go because I'm cured. But I never want to see your hairy little legs in Agrabah again. Understand?"

The bug spun around once and took off.

"No sense of humor," said the Genie. "And one more thing—I never want to lay eyes on that robe again. As a fashion statement, it's a joke."

"Why not leave it here for Hamoud? With a good washing, the robe will serve him better than that old blanket," Aladdin said. "The important thing is, you're back to normal, Genie."

"No stick, no ick," said the Genie. "Just

one big dry guy, at your service."

"Thank goodness for that," said Aladdin. "Are we ready to head back to the palace now? I know one princess who's going to be happy when she sees you."

"I can hardly wait to take her in my arms and hug her and squeeze her —"

"Easy, Genie. After this adventure, you'd better be on your best behavior for a while." Aladdin laughed.

"Whatever you say, Chief," said the Genie. "I'm big, I'm blue, and I'm back!"